Created by
Jim Jinkins

CHRONICLES

Poor Roger

Story by Bill Gross and Linda K. Garvey

Illustrated by
Matthew Maley, William Presing, Tony Curanaj, John
Brandon, and Zigang (Ziggy) Chen

Poor Roger is hand-illustrated by the same
Grade A Quality Jumbo artists who bring you
Disney's Doug, the television series.

New York

Created by
Jim Jinkins

Poor
Roger

CHAPTER ONE

The sun rose over the Poulet Mountains. Roger Klotz looked out the window of his room at the great view south of Bluffington. He looked at the luxurious neighborhood of Boogerton Heights where he lived. He looked at his own richly landscaped property, and he admired the topiary of himself looking sassy in the front yard.

He felt like the luckiest guy in the world. "What a great day to be me!"

Stinky, his cat, napped at the foot of the bed. "Yawn," she replied. She didn't care what he said, as long as she got her daily bowl of Tuna Diddlies.

Roger turned back to the view. From his mansion, he could see past Lucky Duck Lake almost all the way to Bloatsburg where his dad lived. "Rats!" Roger groaned.

Roger's dad was a clown. A real circus clown—big red nose, floppy shoes, the whole deal. Every time

he thought about his dad getting
smacked in the face with cream
pie and squirted down the pants
with seltzer, he got embarrassed.
Worst of all, a clown barely made
enough money to pay the rent.
What a loser! thought Roger.

And now, his dad was coming to visit. He'd probably take Roger to eat at the corniest lunch spot in Bluffington—Clowny's Clowneteria! Deep down, Roger wanted to see his dad, sort of, but he sure hoped nobody saw him hanging out with a real clown!

Roger watched as Ned, Willy, and Boomer crossed his big front lawn, past the old trailer he used to live in. Willy rang the doorbell. Roger yelled out the window. "All right, already! I'll be down in a minute. Hold your horses!"

Roger smiled. He'd make them wait a few minutes for no reason. Having that power made him feel like a big shot.

CHAPTER TWO

"Roger! Breakfast! Come and get it!" shouted his mom, Edwina. Roger smelled the frying eggs and weenies as he walked into the kitchen. Even though it was his favorite breakfast, he put on a fake frown.

"Mom!" he whined. "That's not what I wanted! I asked you to

serve me those French snails I saw in *Rich Guy Magazine*!"

"Oh, Roger," said Edwina, "you know you don't want snails. And besides, they're way too expensive." Roger wanted his mother to cook fancy gourmet foods now that they could afford it, but she still liked cooking the same old food they ate before they got rich.

"You know what, Roger?" she added. "I don't know much about fancy food, but I know that *nothing* smells better than fried weenies in the morning! Now, come on and eat." She smiled, handed him a plateful, and watched him scarf it down.

"Okay, so this *does* taste good,"
he admitted. "But don't forget,
we're having sushi tonight," Roger
demanded, pointing at another
picture from *Rich Guy Magazine*.
"Except, this time, make sure you
cook it good, okay?"

"Well, I'll give it a whirl, Roger,

but this isn't what I do best," his mother told him.

Edwina Klotz was a proud woman. She had become a hairdresser at Rose's Unisex Beauty Salon for Men and Women straight out of high school. She could have quit her job after she sold her trailer lot in Fat Jack's Trailer Park to Bill Bluff. Bluff had already built the new middle school on that land, so he had to pay a ton of money for it. Edwina didn't need to work now. In fact, she could have bought Rose's Salon and called it Edwina's, but she decided to keep her job just the way it was.

"When are you gonna quit that

lame-o job, Edwina?" Roger liked to call his mother by her first name. It made him feel grown-up.

"Hon," Edwina replied, "I love my job and I'm good at it. I'll always work at Rose's."

"Well, I don't think the mother of the Great Roger Klotz should be messing around with other people's hair," Roger complained. "Everybody knows that a rich guy's mom doesn't work."

"Well, this one does," she declared, "although I am thinking of taking a few days off to redecorate this monstrosity of a house. I want to make it feel more homey. What do you think, son?"

Roger looked shocked. "Monstrosity! Mom, what do you mean? I *love* this place! It's so show-off-y, it makes me feel like . . . like a rich guy."

She ruffled his hair. "Don't you worry about it, hon. I think I know how to make this mansion sit up and say, 'Hey!

I'm the home of Roger and Edwina Klotz!'"

"Yeah, that's what I'm afraid of," Roger muttered. "You'll ruin it, and then what will people say?"

Outside a car honked, TOOT-TOOT!

"They'll say that those Klotzes are plain ol' down-to-earth folks. Now run along, sweetie. Your limo's waiting." She kissed Roger on the forehead. "Love you."

Roger got embarrassed. "Maa-ommm!"

CHAPTER THREE

Roger's gang was still waiting when he came out the door. "Duh, gee, Roger," complained Willy. "What took you so long?"

"None of your beeswax! The rich and powerful Klotz answers to no one!" he announced to his friends. "And don't you forget it! I'm rich! R-I-C-K-H, rich, and what I say, goes."

"Then say we'll go somewhere really cool today, Rog. How about Funkytown?" asked Boomer.

"Yeah! And let's stop at Swirly's on the way," Ned chimed in.

"Yeah, Rog. Duh, since you got so much money, how about we go see the new Dr. Cop movie, your treat?" suggested Willy. The gang always had big plans for spending Roger's money.

CHAPTER FOUR

From his booth at Swirly's, Doug watched as Roger and his gang got out of the limousine. "Hey, look," he said to Skeeter, Patti, and Beebe in the booth with him. "Looks like Roger's been shopping."

Willy, Ned, and Boomer carried stacks of packages so high they couldn't see where they were going. Roger directed them loudly into the booth next to Doug's.

"Hey, you losers! Thought I'd let you see how a rich guy spends his money," Roger announced.

"Hey, Roger," Patti said. "What do you have there?"

"Oh, just a few of the most expensive things money can buy," Roger bragged. "Get a load of these!" he continued. "They cost me a fortune!" He began to open the boxes and bags he had bought. He showed them his new Voice-Activated Underwear Drawer that could choose his underwear on demand and his Fully Automated Nose Blower that would automatically blow his nose when he sneezed.

"Cool, man," said Skeeter, impressed.

"Seems pretty

complicated when all you have to do is open your drawer or blow your own nose," Doug remarked.

Roger explained, "Rich people don't have time to be bothered with stuff like that. We're too busy counting our money. I'll bet you have all of this stuff and more, don't you, Beebe?"

"Well, actually, I wouldn't clutter my elegant space with these little playthings," she answered. "Besides, I have servants."

Roger pulled out the last unopened box. "Okay, then, what about this? You'd have to have a whole team of servants to do what this baby can do. Check it out!" He took out a black case marked MONEY MIZER POCKET COMPUTER.

"Boring!" Beebe was still disinterested.

"You wish!" Roger responded. He opened up the Money Mizer. While they waited for him to find the ON button, Beebe turned to Patti and said, "So, speaking of changing the subject—"

"Hold it!" Roger yelled. "You'll miss it."

"Really, Roger," Beebe said, annoyed. "I don't care about your little toy! I have *IMPORTANT* things to discuss! Now leave us alone."

"Oh, excuse me, *Miss* La-Dee-Dah, for taking up so much of your valuable time! I guess you don't need to know how a REALLY rich guy manages his money," he taunted her.

"Oh, all right! But this better be good, Roger Klotz, or it's the last time I give you the time of day!"

Everyone watched as the little computer came to life. Suddenly it beeped and said, "Working." Lights blinked and the voice said, "For money transactions, press 1. For balance information . . . " The Mizer listed options and Roger typed responses. Doug suggested, "Maybe you ought to read the

instructions
first, Roger."

"Yeah, what
if it calls the
police on you,
Rog," joked
Ned.

"Duh, do
you think it can order take-out
pizza?" asked Willy.

"Pipe down, you lunkheads."
Roger snapped. "This thing is
factory-programmed to anticipate
my every financial need. It's even
better than having servants,
Beebe! Now, everybody shut up,
so I can hear."

The computer spoke: "Roger M.

Klotz, Esquire, Account
Summary: Wow! Are you loaded!!"

Roger was in heaven. "See, you goofballs. I'm rich and the really rich get really richer. Right, Beebe?"

"Good grief," Beebe sighed. "It's enough to make me wish for bankruptcy . . . yours, of course!"

"Hardy har har!" Roger replied. "I'll show you how to make money. Watch this."

The computer beeped again and a moment later, Roger pushed a big red button.

Suddenly, an earsplitting alarm went off, and the computer voice shouted, "Fatal Error F-28!"

Roger's joy quickly turned to panic. "Aaaaghhh! Fatal Error F-28!" he screamed. "Look what you made me do!!"

"What's 'Fatal Error F-28?'" asked Doug.

"How should *I* know?" Roger said. "Who's got time to read all this?!!" He handed Doug the huge instruction manual.

Patti, Skeeter, and Beebe watched helplessly as Doug looked up "Fatal Error F-28" in the manual's index. A few seconds later, he stopped. "Uh-oh," he said, looking nervously at Roger.

Roger panicked. "What! WHAT! **WHAT**!" he hollered.

Doug replied, " 'Fatal Error F-28' means 'Delete All Money.' I guess you're broke, Roger."

CHAPTER FIVE

Broke! Roger thought to himself, this can't be happening! This was worse than being poor in the first place. Now, not only was he broke, but he had to face the pity of everyone he knew. No, no, **NO**! This just couldn't be happening!

What could he do? If only the last few minutes had not taken place. If only he had read the instructions and not pushed that big red button. If only—if only—

A loan, that's what he needed—a BIG loan. Who did he know who had that kind of money?

"Beebe," he said, turning toward her. "I don't suppose you would lend me a small fortune? I'm good for—"

"What?!!" she squawked. Then she laughed out loud. "Ha, ha! Me loan *you* money? Yeah, right. Like I would voluntarily hand over *my* family's precious fortune. How do you think we got to be the richest family in town? Not by forking over my daddy's hard-earned cash to poor people like you!"

Humiliated, Roger steamed out of Swirly's, heading toward home. As he walked, his brain dove into a horrible nightmare of a day-dream.

Two clowns performed on the streets of downtown Bluffington. They were dressed in raggedy clothes and big floppy shoes with holes in the bottoms. Their pockets were turned inside out, empty. The big clown chased the smaller clown with a bottle of seltzer, while the smaller one ran from him, holding a big fluffy cream pie in his hand. Roger saw that the big clown was his father. He wondered who the small one was.

"I've got you now!" the big clown said as he caught up to the small one. As he grabbed the little clown by the pants and squirted seltzer down them, the little one twisted around and smashed his cream pie into the big clown's face.

"Oh, good shot, son!" said the big clown. Suddenly, with a sick, sinking feeling in the pit of his stomach, Roger knew who the small clown was. He was Roger!

CHAPTER SIX

When Roger ran out of Swirly's, he forgot all his expensive gadgets. "Wow," said Doug, "he must be VERY upset."

"Yeah," Patti added. "I've never seen him so upset that he couldn't even call us losers or anything. What should we do?"

"Do?" said Beebe. "What's there

to do? His mom will get some more money from the bank."

"Uh, Beebe, I don't think he can do that," explained Skeeter. "I think their money's all gone."

Beebe looked confused. "I'm sorry. I can't imagine that."

"Oh, well," said Ned. "Easy come, easy go. Guess we have to find another meal ticket . . . Say, Beebe—"

"Get real," Beebe shrugged.

"Duh, let's get out of here," Willy added, as the gang ran out the door.

"Well, we can't just leave his stuff here," Doug said. "Let's take it back to his house."

"Good idea, Doug. Come on, Beebe," said Patti, handing her a small package.

"Well, okay," Beebe replied, "but I hope this doesn't make me sweaty."

The four kids took Roger's new things and headed for Boogerton Heights.

"Hey there, kids!" Edwina called, overtaking them. "Heading over to Beebe's house?"

"No, Mrs. Klotz," Patti answered. "We're on our way to *your* house."

"Yes, Mrs. Klotz," Doug added. "We're really sorry about you losing your money and all—"

"My money? Why, whatever are you talking about, Doug?" Edwina asked.

Doug stammered, realizing she

had no idea what had happened. Soon, all the kids were trying to explain at once. Edwina was relieved when she learned that Roger was okay and he was only upset because he lost their money.

"Yeehaw!" she said happily. "Maybe now that boy can quit worrying about all that money and start having fun."

She thought for a moment. "Oh, goodie, we'll get to move back into the trailer again. It's a good thing we hung on to it! I never really liked that big ol' house, anyway. Too fancy!"

CHAPTER SEVEN

When Roger got home from
Swirly's, his dad was waiting on
his doorstep. Dressed in his clown
suit, Roger's dad waved his arms
and shouted, "Why, there's a kid
so bright, I think I'll call him
'son'! Get it? Son? Sun? HA HA!"
Even for a clown, Roger's dad was
loud.

Great, thought Roger. This is just what I need.

"Hey, Roger," Mr. Klotz continued, smiling. "What does a ghost wear to a party?"

"Please, Dad, no jokes," Roger pleaded.

"Boo jeans!" his dad laughed loudly. "Get it? Ghost? Boo? HA HA!" Roger groaned.

"Dad," Roger said, "I just lost my money and I don't feel like joking." He explained what had happened that afternoon.

When Roger finished, his dad hugged him and said, "Son, I know how you must feel. But it could have been worse—"

"No offense, Dad," Roger cut him off, "but you're a clown. How could you know what losing a fortune feels like?"

"Roger, having money doesn't make you important and it can't make you happy." Roger's dad was speaking very seriously. "Liking yourself, liking other people— those things will make you happy.

"I'm a clown," he continued, "and I know that embarrasses you. But I like it. So do other folks. After all, it's who you *are* that matters, not what you have!"

Roger spoke up. "You know what, Dad? It's hard to take you seriously in that goofy hat and big red nose."

There was a moment of silence. Then they both laughed.

Roger's dad said, "Tell you what, why don't you come stay with me a week in Bloatsburg while things settle down here? We've got a lot of catching up to do."

Roger thought for a moment. "What about Mom?" he asked. "I

lost all her money. I can't just leave her here."

"Well, I can give you a check that should hold you over for now. I don't have a fortune, but whatever I've got, I'll be happy to share." With that, Roger's dad made out a check that was almost enough to cover the next month's mortgage payment.

Suddenly Roger had a big lump in his throat. When he spoke again, he sounded hoarse. "Gee, Dad, uh . . . thanks," he said, holding back a tear. "Oh, for cryin' out loud! I got dust in my eye . . . or something."

CHAPTER EIGHT

On Monday morning, while Roger
was in Bloatsburg, Edwina called
the bank. The manager assured
her that their money was safe
and sound. Since Roger didn't
read the instructions on his Mizer
computer, he didn't know how to
connect it to his bank accounts.
The big red button was only good

for making an earsplitting alarm.

When Roger didn't show up for school, Doug, Skeeter and Patti were worried. They walked over to Rose's Salon after school to find out where he was.

Edwina was sweeping up when they arrived. Above the mirror in her booth, a large Bluffco bumper sticker read, HAIRDRESSERS ♥ TO TEASE. She told them Roger was spending the week with his father and the money was safe. They were thrilled to hear the news!

Doug said, "Gee, Mrs. Klotz, I guess that means you have to stay in your fancy house."

"Doug," she said, "I may have to stay there, but it doesn't have to stay fancy. It's time to redecorate!"

"Boy, I bet Roger'll be surprised," said Patti.

"Hey!" Doug exclaimed. "Why don't we have a welcome-home party for Roger? I still remember what a great surprise party you and Roger threw for my one-year anniversary of moving to Bluffington. The food was great! And it made me feel like people liked me. Maybe Roger needs to know that right now."

Edwina loved the idea. "You know, Doug, I think you're right. A surprise welcome-home party sounds like just the thing! Let's see, now, what'll we have . . . "

CHAPTER NINE

When Roger reached his mansion,
the front door was locked, so he
had to ring the bell. The door
popped open. "Hey," he said,
"what's going on?"

All of a sudden, "Surprise!!!" All
his friends popped out from
hiding places everywhere—inside
closets, behind doors, under

tables, behind curtains. They
started to cheer, hoot and whistle.
Everyone was there—Patti,
Beebe, Skeeter, Chalky, and
Roger's gang. Even Judy Funnie
made a special guest appearance.

"Welcome home!" they all
yelled.

From the living room ceiling, a giant sign bounced down. It said, WELCOME HOME, ROGER! Confetti shot through the air.

"Joeycookamonga!" he exclaimed.

And the food! There was food everywhere. It was all of Roger's favorite party snacks: Weenies-in-a-Blanket, Weenies Olé, Casserole à la Weenie, Swedish Weenie Balls, and for dessert, Weenies Flambé!

Roger stopped in his tracks. "Hey, hold everything! What happened here?"

"Surprise again!" said Edwina, leading him over for a better look

at the new furnishings. "I
decorated it to look just like our
old trailer! What do you think?"

Roger looked around the room.
Edwina, Doug, and all the kids
waited breathlessly. "I don't like it
. . ." he finally answered.

Edwina's face fell. Roger continued, " . . . I *love* it!" Everybody cheered and Edwina smiled so big, her makeup almost cracked.

Roger looked around at all of his friends, amazed. "You all did this for a poor guy?" he asked.

"You're *not* poor, Roger!" Beebe blurted out.

Roger groaned. "Oh, no! Not another speech about how you don't need money to be rich!" he whined.

"No," Patti explained, "you're *still* rich!"

Skeeter added, "Yeah, the red button on your computer wasn't hooked up yet. You didn't lose a penny!"

Roger replied, "Ah-ha! So you did all this 'cause I'm rich!"

Doug rolled his eyes. "Don't you get it, Roger? We don't care if you're rich or not. It's what you are on the inside that counts."

"Yeah, Roger, just because you're obnoxious doesn't mean you're not our friend," Skeeter added.

Roger said, "Yeah! And just because you're all a buncha weenies doesn't mean you can't be *my* friends!"

Everybody laughed and Doug said, "Speaking of weenies, let's eat!"

CHAPTER TEN

The next morning as the sun rose again over the Poulet Mountains, Roger Klotz looked out the window of his room. He thought about what a great mom he had. He thought about all his great friends, and he thought about his dad, too, and this time he didn't groan.

Roger felt like the luckiest guy in the world. "What a great day to be me!"

Stinky yawned and started thinking about Tuna Diddlies.